'For my mother, my child's mother, and every mother in the world.'
- Aftab Yusuf Shaikh

Letters to Ammi

First Reprint March 2020

Text: Aftab Yusuf Shaikh
Photographs: Adrija Ghosh and Soumitra Ranade
Drawings: Aparna Trikkur

email: contact@karaditales.com
www.karaditales.com

ISBN: 978-81-9338-893-8

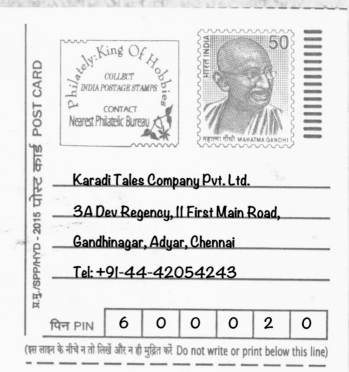

POST CARD

Philately: King Of Hobbies
COLLECT
INDIA POSTAGE STAMPS
CONTACT
Nearest Philatelic Bureau

भारत INDIA 50

महात्मा गांधी MAHATMA GANDHI

प्र.मु./SPP/HYD - 2015 पोस्ट कार्ड

Karadi Tales Company Pvt. Ltd.

3A Dev Regency, II First Main Road,

Gandhinagar, Adyar, Chennai

Tel: +91-44-42054243

पिन PIN   6 0 0 0 2 0

(इस लाइन के नीचे न तो लिखें और न ही मुद्रित करें Do not write or print below this line)

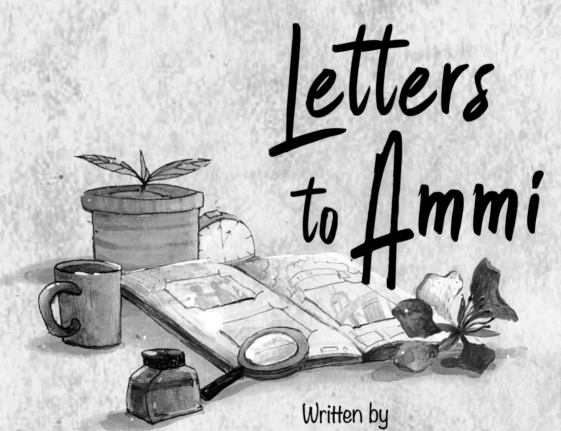

Letters to Ammi

Written by
Aftab Yusuf Shaikh
Photographs by
Adrija Ghosh and Soumitra Ranade

Dear Ammijaan,

I have arrived in your city. It has taken seven hours to get here from Jaipur.
It is still early in the morning and there is a nip in the air.

I read the big yellow sign that says Hazrat Nizamuddin again and again,
wondering if this is just a dream. People are pouring out of the train and
scrambling away. I walk slowly, tracing the railing of the foot overbridge with
my fingers. I wonder if you held on to it each time you returned to Delhi after
visiting Abbu's relatives in Jaipur.

Abbu told me all about the places that you love in Delhi. Now, I look forward
to seeing them for myself. Will it feel like two Delhis (or Dillis as you would
have said) - one that Abbu described for me and the one that I will see?
I spot Khaalu waiting for me.

Your daughter,
Fatima

Dear Mumma,

I am struck by Khaalu's warmth, even though I haven't seen him in years. He has a salt and pepper beard now, and wears a felt hat. He asked me about my exams, which I somehow passed. When school reopens, I will join class eight. Yes, that's right - your little girl is in class eight now!

He can't believe I came all the way from Jaipur on my own. Truth be told, neither can I. Abbu asked me to wait for two days so that he could accompany me. But as we all know, even setting foot in Delhi is painful for him. I do not want to put him through that. You should have seen how he annoyed poor Khaalu with constant phone calls giving him instructions on when and where to receive me. He dropped me off at the station and didn't move until the train was out of sight.

I stopped Khaalu when he tried to pick up my bag as we walked out of the station.
I said, "Khaalu, please let me handle it. Please!"

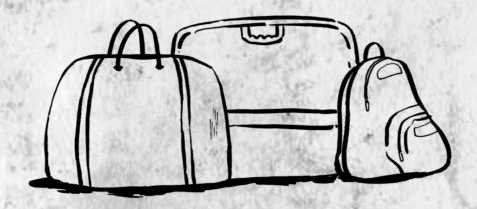

He looked at my face and winked, "After all, you are the daughter of the resolute Mohammad and the fierce Aisha!"

I smiled back, "Yes. I am also from a line of labourers."

Abbu's grandfather was a porter, wasn't he, Ammi? He told me this once. I remember feeling so proud of my forefathers.

We just passed Lodi Gardens in the car! I wanted to stop at your favourite haunt but Khaalu says that Shama Khala has already prepared a big breakfast for me. I can't wait to see her.

The car is constantly being jolted. I should stop writing. Bye for now.

Your daughter,
Fatima

Dear Ammi,

After a quick breakfast, Khala took me to shop for salwar kameez fabrics. Chandni Chowk has so many shops and so many people, I have to dance around like a brinjal on a heated pan!

I see a stall selling ribbons and I think of Abbu. He always ties my pigtails with ribbons early in the morning. He even wakes up at dawn to make me breakfast. Still, I wish you could braid my hair or make my favourite dishes. Khala says there's a lane somewhere around here from where you bought your black and crimson dress for your high school farewell party. In Delhi, you call it a send-off, right?

That dress is still kept at home, carefully preserved. Abbu does not let me touch it. He says he will present it to me when I turn seventeen. I want to be the kind of daughter who is worthy of a mother like you. Abbu has never cared about not having a son – he's proud of being my father, and I will not let him down.

Your daughter,
Fatima

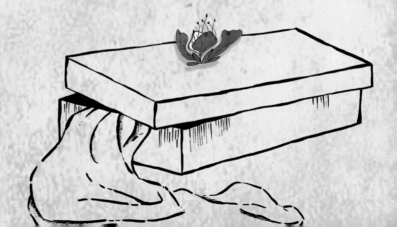

Ammi,

I have heard stories of how you were scared of dark water and wells. Aunty has brought me to Rajon Ki Baoli, this very strange stepwell with all its green water and an ominous appearance. I have inherited your fears too, I feel. Khala tells me how the two of you came here the day before you left for Mumbai to meet Abbu.

The whole place is quiet and eerie, hidden deep in the outskirts of the city. I took a picture of myself with Khala at the exact same place where you sat with her.

Your loving daughter,
Fatima

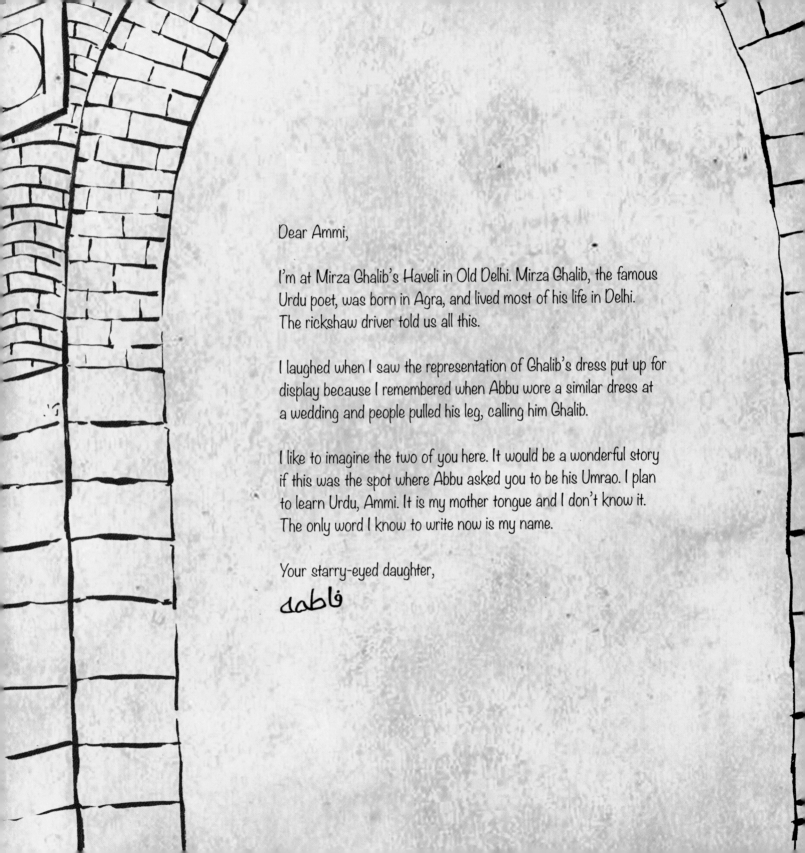

Dear Ammi,

I'm at Mirza Ghalib's Haveli in Old Delhi. Mirza Ghalib, the famous
Urdu poet, was born in Agra, and lived most of his life in Delhi.
The rickshaw driver told us all this.

I laughed when I saw the representation of Ghalib's dress put up for
display because I remembered when Abbu wore a similar dress at
a wedding and people pulled his leg, calling him Ghalib.

I like to imagine the two of you here. It would be a wonderful story
if this was the spot where Abbu asked you to be his Umrao. I plan
to learn Urdu, Ammi. It is my mother tongue and I don't know it.
The only word I know to write now is my name.

Your starry-eyed daughter,

dabló

Dear Ammi,

Khala and I had an amazing late lunch at Bengali Sweet House.
We ordered chole bhature and ghee laddoos - your favourite combination!

Abbu is a very protective (maybe a little too protective) father. He called
Khala even though he's spoken to me twice after the train reached Delhi.
I know he's missing me, so I will send him a postcard.

Once, when I opened Abbu's drawer, I saw all the postcards you had
sent him. There was this black-and-white one with your face mostly
covered by your shiny hair. At first, I thought it was some gorgeous
movie star. People comment that I look like you, but I disagree.

Your daughter,

Fatima

Mamma,

Khala has been obsessed with showing me around Delhi.
We are here now at Nizamuddin. I have read a lot about
this dargah. The great Brij poet Amir Khusrao is buried
here, as is the noble saint Hazrat Nizamuddin.

Ammi, also buried here is a woman who used to intrigue
you in your teenage years -
Malika-e-Hindustan Padshah Jahanara Begum.
I have seen paintings of her and found her to be lovely.
And because you liked her, she has become fascinating
to me as well.

Love you,
Fatima

Dear Ammijaan,

We are sitting on a bench. The Qutub Minar rises to the sky in front of us! Khala tells me that out of all the places in Mehrauli, this one is her favourite. She tells me about the conversations the two of you had sitting on this very bench. It must have taken you a lot of courage to talk to your parents about wanting to marry Abbu.

Khala takes my palm and kisses it. Her eyes are wet. She smiles and says, "You are your mother's daughter." Fourteen years later, this bench, once half-shared by you, is now half-shared by me.

My mother's daughter,
Fatima

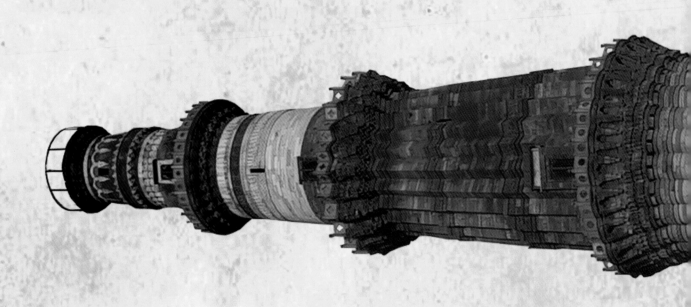

Dear Mother,

I feel a slight chill in the air again as I sit on the steps of
the Jama Masjid.

When Emperor Shah Jahan built this mosque (when he got it
built, I mean), he must have marvelled at the finished building.
The Taj Mahal is only a symbol of love, but this is a symbol
of worship. I like simplicity and utility. The Taj Mahal is gorgeous,
but it is of no use to the common man. In fact, it sometimes
embarrasses husbands before their wives, Abbu likes to joke.

I tell you, Ammi, a view from the top of this mosque's minaret feels like you are balancing on a cloud. And from the narrow staircase, you can see the whole of Delhi and feel like a Mughal emperor, or empress in my case.

I can't find the words to explain how it felt when I reached the top of the minaret. Did you feel the same way when Abbu brought you here?

Your humble daughter,
Fatima

Your Highness,

I'm relaxing on a lawn, sipping apple juice.

Right in front of me is the building that housed the throne of the Emperor of India. I wonder how those days must have been when people flocked to this Diwan-e-Aam and put forth their requests and complaints before their ruler. I think of grandfather and how scandalised he would have been when a boy from a humble background came to ask for the hand of his daughter.

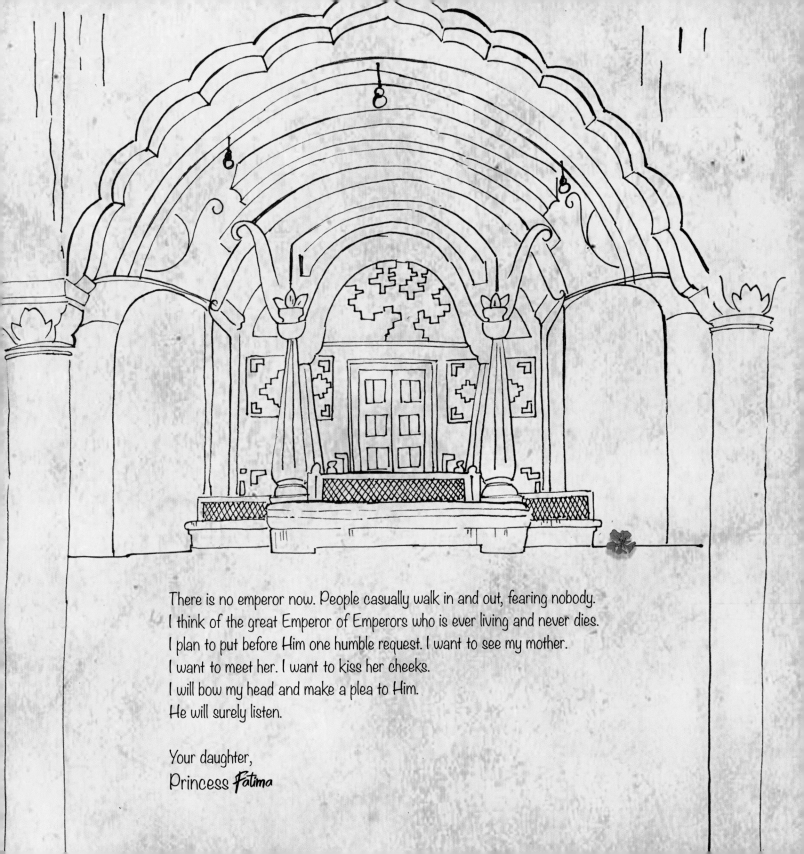

There is no emperor now. People casually walk in and out, fearing nobody.
I think of the great Emperor of Emperors who is ever living and never dies.
I plan to put before Him one humble request. I want to see my mother.
I want to meet her. I want to kiss her cheeks.
I will bow my head and make a plea to Him.
He will surely listen.

Your daughter,
Princess Fatima

Beloved Ammi,

We meandered through a tangle of roads and halted at an old iron gate that is painted moss green. I am told this is the Panj Peeran Graveyard where you rest. I can't stop staring at your grave. All the other graves are decorated with marble or flowers or lime, but not yours. You are simple even in death.

I am so close to you but still cannot meet you or kiss your cheeks. I can't hold you or hug you. I can't even fight with you. All my friends and cousins can fight with their mothers because they can apologise later. But between you and me, the bridge of forgiveness has fallen. Ammi, I know I shouldn't cry, but my heart is breaking, and my eyes are so full of tears, I am blinded by them.

Ammi, I am going back home. I don't want to come back. I now know why Abbu never comes to Delhi. Every place in this city shows me how full of life you were, and then it reminds me that you are gone.
Bye, Ammi. Khuda Hafiz.

خدا حافظ

Your daughter and reflection,
Fatima

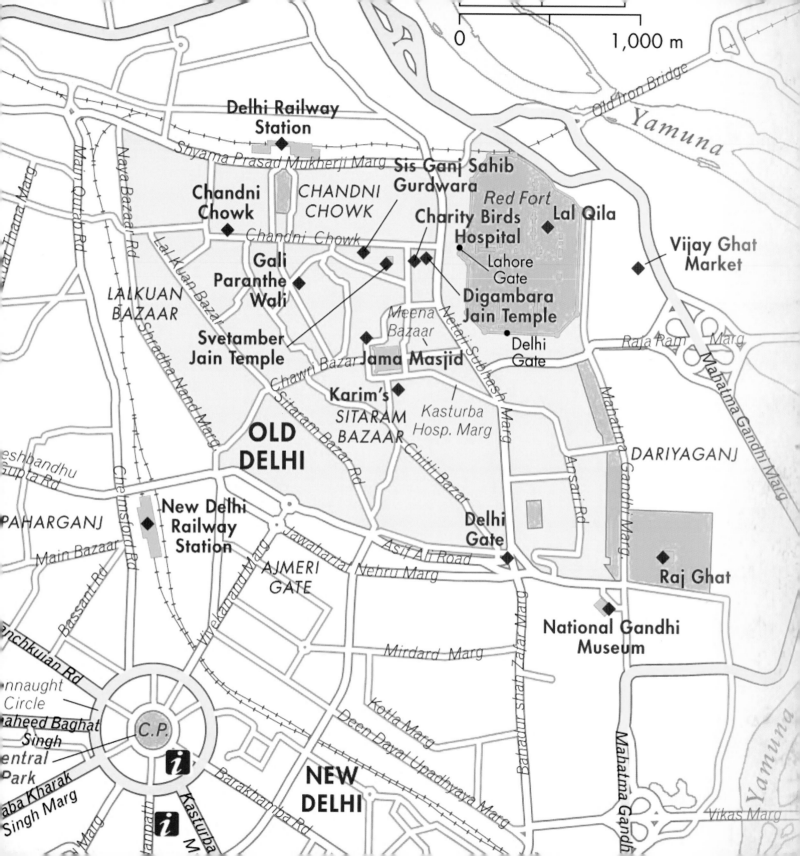

DISCOVER DELHI

Delhi is a hypnotic melting pot of cultures and languages - a thriving modern city that is as passionate about development as it is about preserving its colourful history. Home to Asia's largest spice market - Khari Baoli, and one of India's best-known handicrafts bazaars – Dilli Haat, and dotted with architectural masterpieces that are nearly a thousand years old, the city is a perpetual muse for poets, filmmakers, artists, and writers.

Inaugurated as the capital of India in 1931, the city's imposing political buildings include the Rashtrapati Bhavan (President's Residence) – the largest residence of any head of state in the world, the Central Secretariat on Raisina Hill, and the iconic Parliament House whose circular structure is inspired by the Ashoka Chakra that appears on the national flag.

Raj Ghat, the memorial dedicated to Mahatma Gandhi, is a prominent Delhi landmark. The memorials of several Indian prime ministers, including Jawaharlal Nehru, Indira Gandhi, and Lal Bahadur Shastri, are in this area that is landscaped by trees planted by visiting political dignitaries. India Gate, formerly the All India War Memorial, is a tribute to the 70,000 soldiers who lost their lives in the First World War, and is believed to have been inspired by the Arc de Triomphe in Paris.

Delhi is one of the best performing metropolitan economies in the world, and is said to have one of the world's best rapid transit systems. It is estimated that Delhi will be the most populous city in the world by 2028.

Jama Masjid

As the largest mosque in India, Jama Masjid can accommodate as many as 25,000 people at a time. The word 'Jama' refers to the prayers offered on Fridays by Muslims. The ornate structure is made of red sandstone and white marble, and took 12 years, five thousand workers, and one million rupees to build. Construction of the mosque began in the 17th century by Mughal emperor Shah Jahan who also commissioned the Taj Mahal in Agra.

Adrija Ghosh

Red Fort

Considered a stellar example of Mughal architecture, the Red Fort (also referred to as Lal Qila) is the site where Jawaharlal Nehru, India's first Prime Minister, hoisted the national flag to celebrate the country's independence from colonial rule on August 15, 1947: a tradition that continues to this date. In 2007, the Red Fort was declared a UNESCO World Heritage site. The Diwan-e-Aam (translates to Hall of Public Audience) is one of the most well-known structures within the fort and is made of 40 red sandstone pillars.

Soumitra Ranade

Mirza Ghalib Haveli

Mirza Ghalib was one of India's best-known Urdu poets and his ghazals continue to be sung to this day. The mansion (or haveli) in which he died in 1869, has since become a famous tourist destination, with some of his most popular poetry on display, including original manuscripts of these poems. In 1997, the Archeological Survey of India (ASI) declared Ghalib ki Haveli, as it is sometimes called, a Heritage Site.

Adrija Ghosh

Qutub Minar

An iconic monument that is arguably one of the most recognized tourist attractions in New Delhi, the Qutub Minar is 240 feet high, and is the tallest brick minaret in the world. Construction started in 1192, and it was declared a UNESCO World Heritage Site eight centuries later in 1993. In the courtyard of the Quwwat-ul-Islam Mosque, which is near the Qutub Minar and within the Qutub Complex, there is an iron pillar that is popular with visitors who believe that wrapping their arms around it and making a wish will grant them their desire.

Soumitra Ranade

Chandni Chowk

The bustling lanes of this busy market area house shops that stock apparel, food, electronic goods, books, and more, along with famous eating places such as the paratha shops in Paranthewali Gali and the legendary Bikaner Sweet Shop. Chandni Chowk is also home to Khari Baoli, the largest spice market in Asia. This iconic area in Delhi has been featured in various Bollywood movies, and is as popular with tourists as it is with the locals.

Adrija Ghosh

Rajon Ki Baoli

Constructed between the late 15th century and the early 16th century, this medieval stepwell with four levels is situated in the Mehrauli Archaeological Park. With carved ornate arches and rooms on either side at every level, it is believed to be one of Delhi's oldest surviving Baolis. However, the monument is under constant threat of damage on account of reckless practices by tourists, as a result of which it is often found choked with plastic and other waste.

Adrija Ghosh

Mohammed Aftab Yusuf Shaikh is a poet, writer, and teacher based in Mumbai. His writing has been published in a large number of anthologies and journals. He has also published five collections of poetry, the most recent being *Tehzeeb Talkies*, and a novel *The Library Girl*. Aftab has always had a strong connection with Delhi and its history - he believes that every part of the city tells the stories of thousands of people, and that its many layers will always intrigue and excite him.

Adrija Ghosh is a literature graduate from Calcutta who is passionate about illustration. She has been freelancing on illustration and design projects related to book covers, children's books and graphic narratives. She loves to travel, and work with children when she is not illustrating. Her short graphic narrative is now published in *Longform Annual* (a graphic narrative anthology by Harper Collins India).

Soumitra Ranade is an art director, photographer, illustrator, and filmmaker whose films have been screened internationally, including at Cannes. He works in the animation industry. He has written two books for children, both of which take inspiration from his sons' overactive imaginations.